MW01269210

Caution!

When you enter The Red Berry Candy Shop

you are not only walking into our store,

but into our book, and you *could* be in it.

With Love,

Miss Candy

This book is dedicated to...

All children, young and old.

Welcome and I hope you enjoy.

Miss Candy and the Red Berry Candy Shop

Candy Nichols

Read to Me Series

Volume

1

©2017 Candy Nichols. All rights reserved. No part of this publication may be reproduced, distributed, or transmitted in any form or by any means, including photocopying, recording, or other electronic or mechanical methods, without the prior written permission of the author, except in the case of brief quotations embodied in critical reviews and certain other noncommercial uses permitted by copyright law.

ISBN: 978-1-54390-400-0

Before we start the stories of the Red Berry Candy Shop, I would like to tell you about Miss Candy herself. She is the owner/operator of this happy little shop. An older woman who, when asked how old she is, will always reply, "Old enough to know better."

Every morning, as she approaches this wonderful shop, she reaches into her quaint purse and retrieves the key. Then, with the tool in hand, she unlocks and opens the front entrance. As if it were a kitten greeting its beloved owner, a sweet lingering fragrance from the multitude of delicious candies instantly wraps her in a warm embrace. Ah, such a way to start a day.

Next, the dear woman moves on to her morning inspection just to be sure nothing is amiss and all is in its proper place. Her soft eyes carefully scan wooden shelves and barrel baskets, shining jars and colorful bins.

Strangely, as if they've come alive, the rich chocolates bars, gummy, sweets treat and sours, lollipop suckers of all sizes and shapes and flavors seem to perk up and stand at attention for her morning roll call.

When ultimately finding everything in order, Miss Candy—with a wink—will thank the Good Lord for His part and get right to work.

Yet you customers must know no two days are ever the same at The Red Berry. Oh yes, there are those who just need some sweet treat like rich chocolaty fudge or a toasty fireball. But sometimes the proprietor enjoys the fun stories that toddle in right along with the customers, and they bless her greatly.

So, I now will try to remember these stories and place them inside these books for you to find. Because in each child I meet, there's always a wonderful story.

Like the morning, a young man came in with his mother to shop for some yummy delicious treat, perhaps for a good deed he had done. Then, after the carefully chosen purchase was made and the young man was back at the door about to leave, he stopped and turned to deliver some very good advice.

Please,

no Wolves

ALLOWED!!! . . .

Thank you, Miss Candy

"Now if you see a wolf outside...don't open the door and let him in!" To this day Miss Candy follows his advice. Of course, there are no wolves in Northeast Ohio, but if there were, she is now the wiser.

Miss Candy also has her helpers: her granddaughters. For them to work for her they had to learn three simple rules.

1. God is to be first in all decisions.

2. They must make this a happy and special place for everyone who passes through the doors.

3. She insists they have fun.

So, as you read these little stories, stories spun like cotton candy from the heart of this little shop, you may find yourself in one. For you are our stories. Some stories we made up, and some will look just like you. Are you the red-haired little girl with eyes that twinkle when she purchases her chocolate gold coins?

Are you the young man who insists his father is five years old? Maybe, just maybe, you are the one who ran back to the counter after purchasing your treat saying, "Oh, thank you!" with great love in your heart.

Please remember now that, when you walk through these doors, it is you who bless us with your smiles and it is you who we love so much. And because of that, we shall try to tuck a few of you dear folks into these stories here and there and, maybe, just maybe, you will see you.

The Strange Copper Visitor

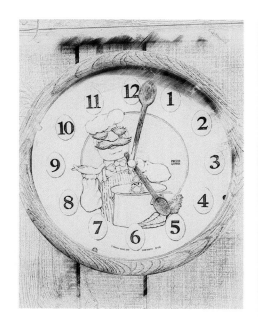

It happened one afternoon about five. That is the time of day Miss Candy calls, "The quiet time." It is when she can usually sit for a while to relax and have a cup of tea while most folks are home enjoying their evening supper. While munching on a celery

stick, she just happened to be chuckling to herself recalling a young lady complaining earlier that morning.

"I have to go to the dentist today," the poor dear girl said in a very solemn voice.

"Why are you so sad?" Miss Candy asked.

"Because I haven't been there in about ten years!"

She was only six.

In an instant Miss Candy heard one of the two customer doors jingle announcing an entering guest. So she stood from her side cove to see who it was. But no one was there!

Now, the way this small but just the right size store is laid out, Miss Candy can see the whole place from her counter. But there was no one, and just to be sure, she looked again, resulting to the same conclusion—no one.

See, if you have ever been there, you would be able to see all around the inside as much as the outside parking spots with large windows wrapped around the front and side of the building. Yet she saw not even a car.

So she settled back down to finish her cup of tea. But as she placed her cup to her lips, she felt as if someone was watching her. She gazed over to the left behind the counter. And then she saw two eyes staring at her.

"Hello," she said.

There he sat on the floor, a little taller than a childs boot with shiny, smooth, copper fur, big brown eyes, and floppy ears... an adorable looking puppy. And the thing was, he just sat there looking at her as if he was saying, "I'm here."

"Oh goodness!" exclaimed Miss Candy.

To which the puppy got up, waddled over, and then plopped down in front of her. *Someone must be pulling a joke on me*, she thought.

"Okay, who's here?" she called. As if whoever brought this puppy in would just pop out laughing...but still, there was no one.

She scooped up the fat-bellied little thing, and as it snuggled right into her, she walked around the store looking again for who had ever delivered such a bundle.

But there was no one.

As she peered deeply into the puppy's eyes, she cuddled him close. "My word, where did you come from?"

To which, he licked the tip of her nose.

He was clean, had no collar, and a full belly.

The rest of the evening, she tried to find out who the owner was. But all to no avail. No one knew anything about this precious puppy, which she nicknamed Copper. She continued asking all the next day, but still, no one had any information.

Until at the end of the day came a young child about eight accompanied by her mother.

Miss Candy greeted them. "Good evening. If you need any help, please just ask."

And then the puppy barked.

"What is that?" The young child perked up, skipping closer.

"That is a sweet puppy someone dropped off here yesterday," Miss Candy said. Then she shared the story about how the puppy came to be and, in finishing the story, let them know she must now find it a home.

The mother and child looked at each other's eyes, saying words with a look only they could understand.

Then the child clasped her hands together. "May I see your puppy?"

"Of course. As long as it is okay with your mom," Miss Candy replied.

"It's fine." the mother murmured, giving a warm smile.

Miss Candy then handed over the little bundle of a puppy, who then plastered the child with puppy kisses. A very excited puppy to be exact, such as Miss Candy hadn't observed till this point.

She stood back in amazement, watching, the loving action between the two.

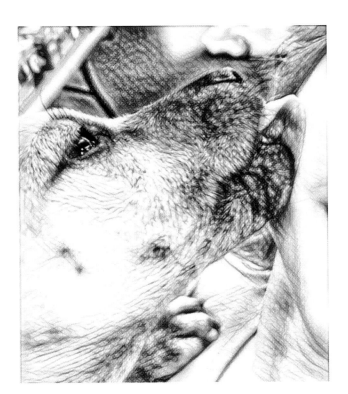

"I must share something, Miss Candy." Still speaking low, as if she revealing a great secret, the mother stepped closer and put her floopy red purse atop the counter.

"Oh?" Miss Candy turned her head to the mother, giving her all of her attention.

"We had just prayed yesterday for a puppy. And we prayed that if God wanted us to have one... that it would be delivered to us in some strange and wonderful way." She paused and gave a little laugh. "And things can't be stranger than a puppy who just shows up. Do you think we could be the home for this puppy?"

Miss Candy looked at the child with the puppy. They were now appearing as inseparable as a chocolate dipped caramel. The two had not stopped loving each other for even a moment.

"Well," Miss Candy couldn't help grinning, "God sure has His wonderful ways in making special things happen. And I am so glad He included me in on this one."

Miss Candy started petting the pup on his head. "So, what do you think you shall call him?"

The child looked around in thought, and then flashed a big, bright grin. "I shall call him Copper!"

"That's perfect!" said Miss Candy, "Because I have been calling him that all along. Copper."

The End